North American edition published by Owlkids Books in 2013.
Translation © 2013 Sarah Quinn
Published in France under the title *Une journée à l'école* © 2012 by Éditions Escabelle.

Owlkids Books acknowledges the financial support of the Canada Council for the Arts, the Ontario Arts Council, the Government of Canada through the Canada Book Fund (CBF) and the Government of Ontario through the Ontario Media Development Corporation's Book Initiative for our publishing activities.

Published in Canada by
Owlkids Books Inc.
10 Lower Spadina Avenue
Toronto, ON M5V 2Z2

Published in the United States by
Owlkids Books Inc.
1700 Fourth Street
Berkeley, CA 94710

Library and Archives Canada Cataloguing in Publication

Cordier, Séverine
    A day at school / by Séverine Cordier and Cynthia Lacroix.

Translation of: Une journée à l'école.
ISBN 978-1-926973-95-1

    1. Vocabulary--Juvenile literature. 2. Word recognition--Juvenile literature. I. Lacroix, Cynthia II. Title.

PE1449.C6513 2013   j428.1   C2012-908496-4

Library of Congress Control Number: 2013930497

Manufactured in Dongguan, China, in February 2013, by Toppan Leefung Packaging & Printing (Dongguan) Co., Ltd.
Job #BAYDC3

A   B   C   D   E   F

Publisher of Chirp, chickaDEE and OWL
www.owlkidsbooks.com

A Day at School

SÉVERINE CORDIER • CYNTHIA LACROIX

Holidays are over!

"May I have a
red pencil case, please?"

pencil case

schoolbag

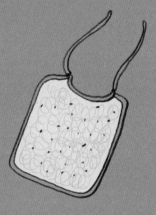

MARKERS

my notebook

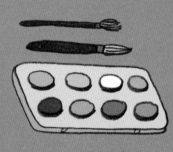

paints

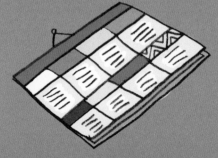

calendar

ballet slippers

"Lift your head up, sweetie!"

PHOTO BOOTH

YOUR PHOTOS IN 3 MINUTES

brushing hair

shaving

tying shoelaces

putting on makeup

making toast

Saying good-bye to Mom and Dad

"What's your name?"

Big kids go to school
and little kids go to day care.

  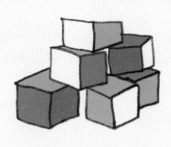

toys

  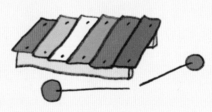

"Welcome, everyone!"

"Oh! This is heavy..."

In the cafeteria

Dreaming

At the playground

"My teacher's name is..."

"Do you want to come over and play?"

Our babysitter
picks us up from school.

"Our favorite snacks!"

Bags packed for
tomorrow

"Dinner's ready!"

"My teacher said..."

All together again

"All done!"